ELMHURST PUBLIC LIBRARY

3 1135 02017 9534

Apr '22 4/0/0

J 921 LEVINE

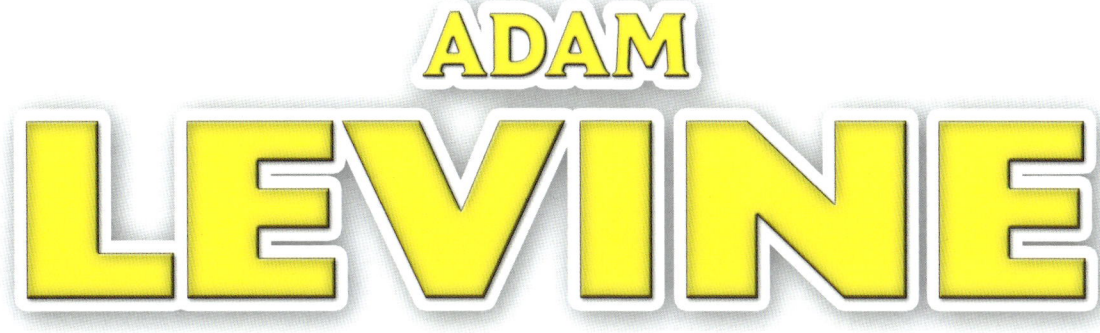

by E. Merwin

Consultant: Starshine Roshell
Music and Entertainment Journalist
Santa Barbara, California

ELMHURST PUBLIC LIBRARY
125 S. Prospect Avenue
Elmhurst, IL 60126-3298

New York, New York

Credits

Cover, © AP Photo/Andrew Harnik; 4, © Kathy Hutchins/Shutterstock; 5, © Featureflashphotographer/Shutterstock; 6, Courtesy Seth Poppel Yearbook Library; 7, © Splash News/Newscom; 8L, Courtesy Seth Poppel Yearbook Library; 8R, © Jon Bilous/Alamy Stock Photo; 9, Courtesy SPG; 10, Courtesy Seth Poppel Yearbook Library; 11, © Everett Collection/Newscom; 12, © Jurij Boiko/Dreamstime; 13, Courtesy SPG; 13 bkgd, © Ricardo Rocha/Dreamstime; 14, © Johan Elzenga/Dreamstime; 15, © Debbie VanStory iPhoto Inc./Newscom; 16, Courtesy SPG; 17, © Mark J. Terrill/AP Photo; 18, © AF Archive/Alamy Stock; 19, © AF Archive/Alamy Stock; 20, © Arindambanerjee/Shutterstock; 21, © Jaguar PS/Shutterstock; 22T, © AF Archive/Alamy Stock; 22B, © Copora/Dreamstime; 23, © Splash News/Alamy Stock Photo.

Publisher: Kenn Goin
Creative Director: Spencer Brinker
Production and Photo Research: Shoreline Publishing Group LLC

Library of Congress Cataloging-in-Publication Data

Names: Merwin, E. author.
Title: Adam Levine / by E. Merwin.
Description: New York, New York : Bearport Publishing, 2019. | Series: Amazing Americans: Pop music stars | Includes bibliographical references and index.
Identifiers: LCCN 2018010850 (print) | LCCN 2018011277 (ebook) | ISBN 9781684027262 (ebook) | ISBN 9781684026807 (library)
Subjects: LCSH: Levine, Adam, 1979—Juvenile literature. | Rock musicians—United States—Biography—Juvenile literature.
Classification: LCC ML3930.L38 (ebook) | LCC ML3930.L38 M37 2018 (print) | DDC 782.42166092 [B] —dc23
LC record available at https://lccn.loc.gov/2018010850

Copyright © 2019 Bearport Publishing Company, Inc. All rights reserved. No part of this publication may be reproduced in whole or in part, stored in any retrieval system, or transmitted in any form or by any means, electronic, mechanical, photocopying, recording, or otherwise, without written permission from the publisher.

For more information, write to Bearport Publishing Company, Inc., 45 West 21st Street, Suite 3B, New York, New York 10010. Printed in the United States of America.

10 9 8 7 6 5 4 3 2 1

CONTENTS

A Hollywood Star 4
LA Baby 6
Kara's Flowers 8
Lucky 222 10
A Dream Come True 12
New Music 14
Maroon 5 16
TV Talent 18
Helping Out 20

Timeline 22
Glossary 23
Index 24
Read More 24
Learn More Online 24
About the Author 24

A Hollywood Star

Fans **shrieked**! Cameras flashed! This time, Adam Levine was not on stage. He was receiving a star on the Hollywood Walk of Fame. Adam thanked his family and fans. "I am me because of you!" he said, smiling.

Adam Levine's star on the Hollywood Walk of Fame

The Hollywood Walk of Fame is 1.3 miles (2.1 km) long. The first star was placed in 1958. Adam got his star in 2017.

LA Baby

Adam Noah Levine was born on March 18, 1979. He grew up in Los Angeles, California. Adam started playing guitar at age ten. Music was the best way for him to express himself. "I picked up a guitar and that was it," Adam said. "I fell so madly in love with it, it's all I did."

When Adam stepped onstage for the first time, he was very nervous. So he performed with his back to the audience!

Adam in seventh grade

As a grown-up, Adam has become a great guitar player. Now, he loves to perform.

Kara's Flowers

At age 15, Adam formed a band with three of his classmates. They named it Kara's Flowers after a girl they all liked. Hundreds of high school kids came to their first show. It was a smash hit! The students loved the band's **original** songs.

Adam, here at age 15, attended the Brentwood School in Los Angeles.

Brentwood is a neighborhood in Los Angeles.

The members of Kara's Flowers included (from left to right): Mickey Madden, Jesse Carmichael, Ryan Dusick, and Adam.

Lucky 222

In 1997, Kara's Flowers made a **demo** at the Room 222 Studio in Hollywood. A few weeks later, the band was playing in Malibu, when a man stopped to listen. He was amazed by the sound. As it turns out, the man was a **producer** who wanted to record the band's first album!

Kara's Flowers at a rehearsal (Adam at center)

Since the demo, Adam believes that 222 is his lucky number. He even tattooed the number on his arm!

A Dream Come True

Adam's dream had come true. Kara's Flowers recorded their first album in 1997. It was called *the fourth world*. The band played many sold-out shows. Adam was on his way to becoming a huge star.

Kara's Flowers used to practice in their drummer's garage!

The album cover for *the fourth world*

New Music

After high school, Adam was ready for an adventure. He drove across the country to the East Coast. Adam loved New York City. He stayed for several years, inspired by the great music there. In 2001, Adam returned to LA to form a new band—Maroon 5.

How did the band choose the name *Maroon 5*? Adam says it's a secret!

New York City

Adam singing with Maroon 5 in 2003

Maroon 5

Maroon 5 quickly put out an album called *Songs About Jane*. It was a hit! The album sold more than 2.7 million copies. Soon after, Adam and the band went on tour. On the road, they made many new fans. In 2005, Maroon 5 won a **Grammy** for Best New Artist!

The cover of Maroon 5's first album, *Songs About Jane*

The members of Maroon 5 include: Jesse Carmichael, Mickey Madden, James Valentine, Adam Levine, and Matt Flynn.

Adam is afraid of flying. As a result, the band often travels by tour bus.

17

TV Talent

Adam has found even more fame on television. Since 2011, Adam has been helping young singers as a coach on *The Voice*. Adam also acted in a spooky TV series called *American Horror Story*.

The Voice is a popular TV show that discovers new singing talent.

Adam in his judge's seat on *The Voice*

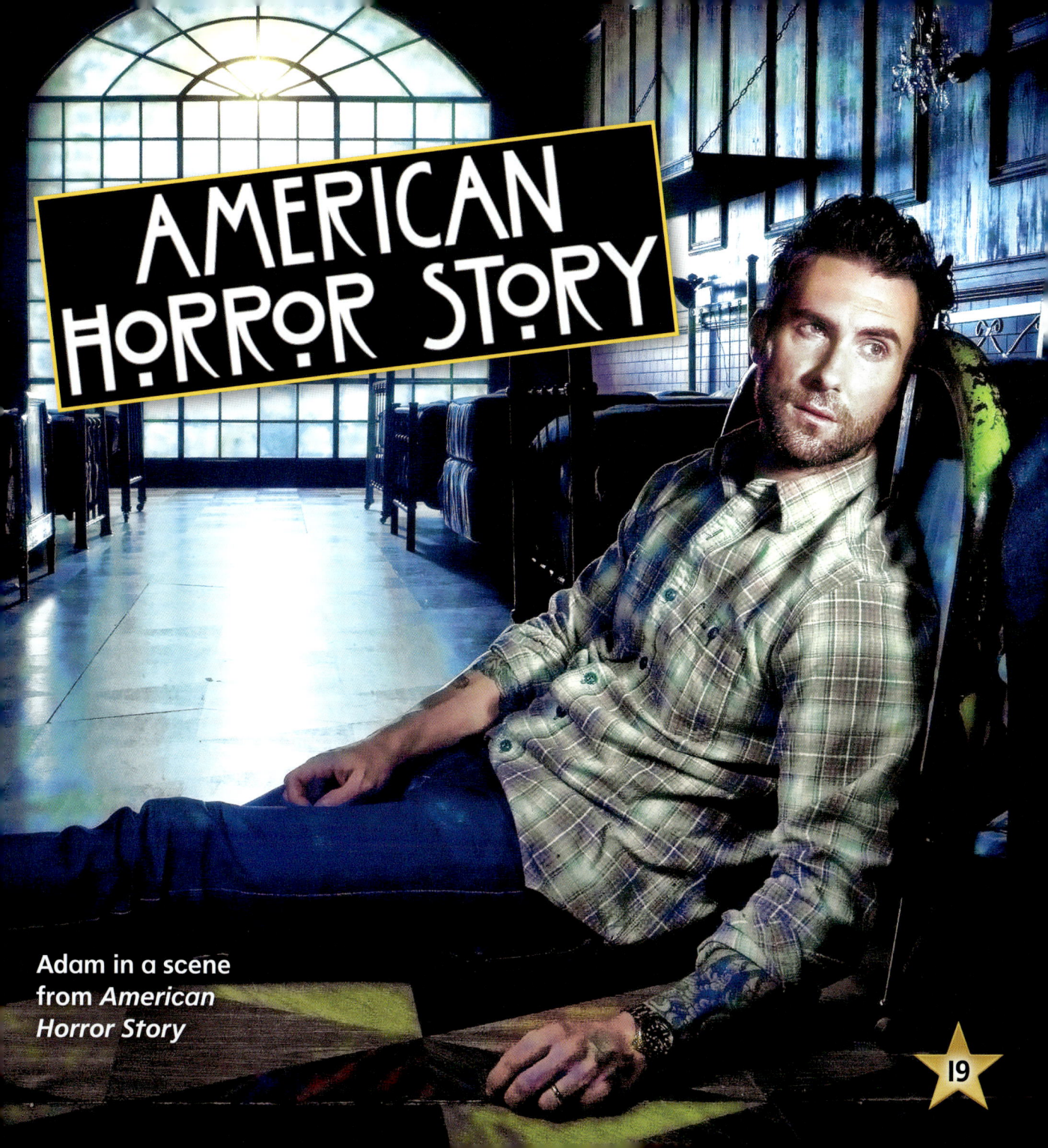

Adam in a scene from *American Horror Story*

Helping Out

Adam also makes time to help others. In 2010, an **earthquake** destroyed much of the island of Haiti. Adam joined 79 other singers to record "We Are the World 25 for Haiti." The song raised money to help Haitians. It's also Adam's way of giving back to a world that has already given him so much!

Haiti after the earthquake

In 2014, Adam married model Behati Prinsloo. They have two daughters, Dusty Rose (seen here) and Gio Grace.

21

Timeline

Here are some key dates in Adam Levine's life.

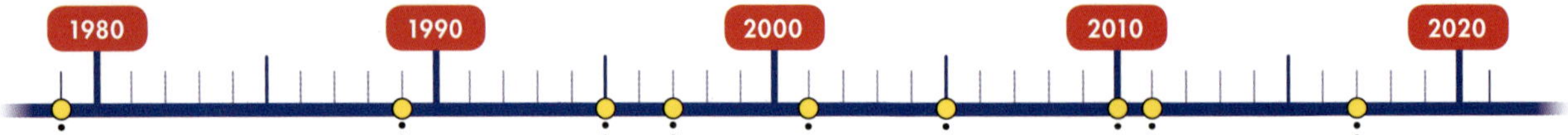

March 18, 1979
Adam Noah Levine is born in Los Angeles, California.

1989
Begins learning to play guitar

1995
Forms his first rock band, Kara's Flowers

1997
Records first album, *the fourth world*

2001
Forms Maroon 5

2005
Maroon 5 wins Grammy for Best New Artist

2010
Helps make "We Are the World 25 for Haiti"

2011
Appears on the first season of *The Voice*

2017
Gets a star on the Hollywood Walk of Fame

Glossary

audience (AW-dee-uhnss) a group of listeners at a concert

demo (DEM-oh) a recording made to show off a performer's talent

earthquake (URTH-kwayk) the sudden shaking of the ground caused by movements of the earth's crust

Grammy (GRAM-ee) an award that recognizes the best music each year

original (uh-RIJ-uh-nuhl) created by an artist, not a copy

producer (pruh-DOO-sir) a person who works with musicians to make records

shrieked (SHREEKT) yelled with excitement

Index

Brentwood School 8
Carmichael, Jesse 9, 16–17
Dusick, Ryan 9
Flynn, Matt 17
fourth world, the 12–13, 22
Grammy Award 16, 22
Haiti 20, 22
Hollywood Walk of Fame 4–5, 22
Kara's Flowers 8–9, 10, 12–13, 22
Madden, Mickey 9, 17
Maroon 5 14–15, 16–17, 22
Prinsloo, Behati 21
Songs About Jane 16
Valentine, James 17
Voice, The 18, 22
"We Are the World 25 for Haiti" 20, 22

Read More

Bankston, John. *Adam Levine (Robbie Readers: Biographies).* Newark, DE: Mitchell Lane (2015).

Tieck, Sarah. *Adam Levine: Famous Singer and Songwriter (Big Buddy Biographies).* Edina, MN: ABDO (2013).

Learn More Online

To learn more about Adam Levine, visit
www.bearportpublishing.com/AmazingAmericans

About the Author

E. Merwin enjoys writing about artists who teach us all to believe in our talents and follow our dreams.